DreamWorks
Trolls
WORLD TOUR

Let's ROCK!

studio fun
INTERNATIONAL

Studio Fun International
An imprint of Printers Row Publishing Group
A division of Readerlink Distribution Services, LLC
10350 Barnes Canyon Road, Suite 100, San Diego, CA 92121
www.studiofun.com

Printers Row Publishing Group is a division of Readerlink Distribution Services, LLC.
Studio Fun International is a registered trademark of Readerlink Distribution Services, LLC.
All notations of errors or omissions should be addressed to Studio Fun International, Editorial Department, at the above address.

ISBN: 978-0-7944-4638-3
Manufactured, printed, and assembled in Heshan, China.
First printing, June 2020. HH/06/20
24 23 22 21 20   1 2 3 4 5

CONTENTS

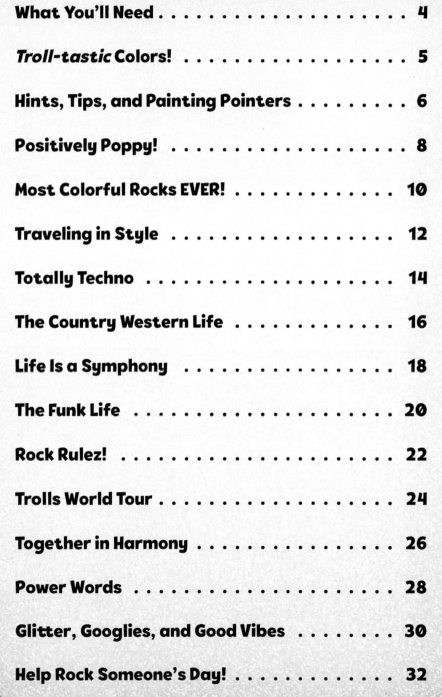

What You'll Need

The Pop Trolls are super crafty, and now you can be, too! This kit has everything you need to turn ordinary rocks into the prettiest decorations ever. Collect all the materials you need before you begin your project.

It's good to be prepared!

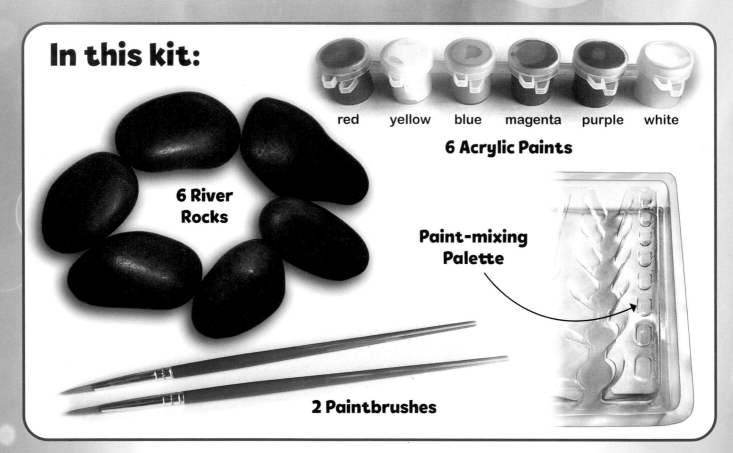

In this kit:

red   yellow   blue   magenta   purple   white

6 Acrylic Paints

6 River Rocks

Paint-mixing Palette

2 Paintbrushes

Things you need from home:

- A few cups or glasses full of water
- Paper towels
- Fine-tipped permanent black marker
- Cotton swabs
- Toothpicks
- Newspaper or other table covering
- Apron or other clothing protector

Extras to make your rocks super special!

- Glitter
- Clear coat spray

Troll-tastic Colors!

This book comes with six paint colors. You can use them to create all the colors needed for the projects in this book. This chart shows you how to mix them. The blister that the paints and rocks come in has special wells you can use as a palette for your paint mixing. Remember to wash and dry your brush after you mix each color.

Each project has a list of colors you'll need to complete it. If a color is in a circle shape, it is one of the paint pot colors. If a color is in a "paint puddle" shape, it is one you need to mix yourself. Use the paint palette in this kit to mix your colors in. Remember, for the projects you can also use any colors you want. Get ready to add *Troll-tastic* colors to your creations!

Fashion starts with color!

Paint Pot Colors   Mixed Colors

Magenta	+	White	=	Pink
Red	+	Yellow	=	Orange
Blue	+	Yellow	=	Green
Blue	+	Purple	=	Dark Blue
Magenta	+ Yellow	+ White	=	Peach
A Touch of	Purple and	Blue	+ White	=	Light Gray
Blue	+ Red	+ White	=	Dark Gray

Hints, Tips, and Painting Pointers

Anyone can paint rocks, and these helpful tips will help you make sure your creations come out *Troll-tastic*! Let's get to it!

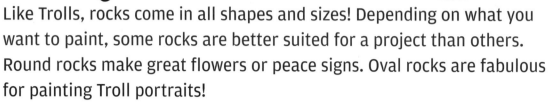

Ready to Rock!

Like Trolls, rocks come in all shapes and sizes! Depending on what you want to paint, some rocks are better suited for a project than others. Round rocks make great flowers or peace signs. Oval rocks are fabulous for painting Troll portraits!

Once you use all the rocks that come with this kit, the fun isn't over. You can use any smooth rocks that you can find around your yard, neighborhood, school, or craft store. You will find the smoothest rocks on beaches or in rivers or streams. Wash and dry rocks before painting.

The paint that comes with this kit is acrylic. If you run out of paint, you can pick up replacements at your local craft store.

The harder the rock, the better!

Getting Started

Before you start painting, ask an adult to use scissors to cut apart the paint pots. This will make them less likely to tip over. An adult should help you open the lids when you are ready to start.

Cover your work area with old newspaper or paper towels, and wear an apron or old shirt to protect your clothes from stains.

Before painting on your rocks, you may want to practice your design or drawing on a piece of paper first. After all, practice makes perfect!

Poppy's Pointers

❀ Most of the time, you will need to paint multiple coats on the rocks to get a consistent color. Let the paint dry between each coat. If you are using cotton swabs or the tip of the brush dipped in paint for a project, you will likely only need to paint once. If you need to make tiny dots, dip the tip of the paintbrush's handle in paint and lightly dab onto the rock.

❀ On average, the paints take between five and ten minutes to dry. Why not work on a second or third project while you wait?

❀ When mixing a new color, test your creation on a piece of paper to make sure you are happy with it before painting the rock.

❀ Make sure you rinse and dry your brushes thoroughly before switching colors.

❀ When your rocks are completely dry, you can spray them with clear coat spray to make them shiny and weatherproof.

Now you are ready to make the cutest, prettiest, happiest rocks ever!

Positively Poppy!

Not only is Poppy the queen of the Pop Trolls, but she is also the queen of crafting. Her scrapbook pages are as bright, fun, and unique as she is. Capture Poppy in all her pink perfection with a craft of your own. Add happiness and positivity to a rock by painting a portrait of Poppy on it!

Colors needed:

Magenta **Pink** **Blue** **Green** **Yellow** **White**

1 Paint a pink circle on the lower half of a rock as shown. You may need two coats.

Life is better with music... and crafts!

3 Use magenta paint to make Poppy's nose and sweet smile. To make her nose, make a dot in the center of her face. Then add a small dot on either side.

2 Paint Poppy's ears by adding two small ovals on either side of the circle as shown. Let dry.

4 Use more magenta paint to make two curvy hair lines on Poppy's head as shown. Add a few more curvy lines to fill in her ponytail as shown. Let dry.

5 Use a cotton swab dipped in paint to add blue and green dots at the base of Poppy's ponytail. This will be her crown! Dip your swab in the paint before making each dot. Let dry.

6 Dip the tip of your paintbrush handle in yellow paint and add tiny dots inside each of the dots that make up the crown. Then add two white circles for her joyful eyes and white freckles as shown. Let dry.

7 Use a black marker to draw eyelashes and pupils, or a toothpick to scratch off the paint to add these black details. Hello, Queen Poppy!

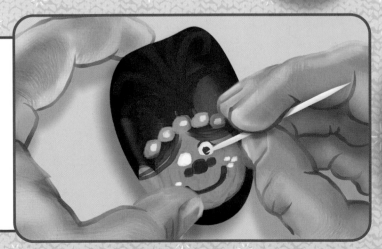

Most Colorful Rocks EVER!

What comes to mind when you think of Trolls Village? There, every day is full of happiness, hugging, music, and lots and lots of color! Bring out your inner Troll with these rock creations that look like they are straight from Poppy's home!

Rainbows Rock!

Colors needed:

Blue **Yellow** **Magenta** **White**

1 Begin your rainbow by painting a blue arch that follows the top edge of your rock.

Oh my Gah!

2 Add a yellow stripe and magenta stripe to your rainbow. You may need more than one coat. Let dry.

High-five worthy!

3 Use a cotton swab dipped in white paint to create a cloud at each end of the rainbow. Add multiple white dots to make the cloud puffy!

Flower Power

Colors needed:

Magenta   Purple   Blue   Green

1   Use a cotton swab dipped in magenta paint to create a large circle made up of dots around the edge of your rock. Let dry.

2   Using purple paint, fill in the center of the flower. The purple should overlap the dots as shown. You may need two coats. Let dry.

3   In the purple center, carefully paint a ring of blue ovals. Make sure to leave space in the center of the ovals.

4   Add a green circle to the center of your beautiful bloom!

Add bling to your bloom with glitter! Sprinkle the glitter over the wet paint, then gently shake the rock to remove the excess glitter.

There is more than one way to paint a flower! Try using seven small rocks to make one big flower. Paint six rocks for petals and one rock to use as the middle. Why not paint lots of little flowers on one rock? What pretty flower designs can you come up with?

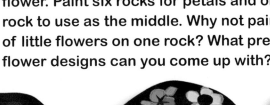

Traveling in Style

What's the best way to get from one end of Trolls Kingdom to the other? Sassy Sheila B., of course! Poppy and her friends wouldn't have been able to unite all the Trolls in harmony without her. Get out your paints and make your very own Sheila B.!

Aw, yeah! Road trip!

Colors needed:

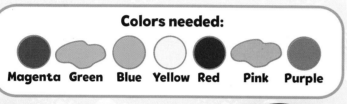

Magenta Green Blue Yellow Red Pink Purple

1 Choose an oval rock for this project. Begin by painting the front of the rock magenta. You may need two coats. Let dry.

2 Use green paint to make a semi-circle in the middle of the rock as shown. This will be Sheila B.'s mouth. You may need two coats. Let dry.

3 Use a cotton swab to make one little blue flower and one little yellow flower at the top of the semi-circle as shown. These will be Sheila B.'s cheerful eyes.

4 Use a black marker or toothpick to make pretty eyelashes and a wide smile as shown. Use the toothpick to scratch away the paint.

5 Use a cotton swab dipped in red paint for Sheila B.'s pupils and her tiny nose.

6 It's time to cover Sheila B. in blooms. Use a cotton swab dipped in yellow paint to make three dots below Sheila B.'s smile. Then, use the tip of your paintbrush handle to add pink and purple dots all over.

7 Finally, use the tip of your paintbrush handle to add two rows of green teeth as shown. Sheila B. is now ready to go!

If you are feeling extra creative, paint a small rock green. This will be Sheila B.'s basket. Then, glue two small pieces of yarn or pipe cleaner to the rocks as shown to connect the basket to the balloon.

Totally Techno

Techno Reef is an LED-lit wonderland where King Trollex keeps the dance party going 24/7! Capture the essence of Techno Reef with these digitally-inspired designs!

Get ready for the drop!

Feel the Heartbeat!

Colors needed:

Magenta   Blue

1 Use a cotton swab dipped in magenta paint to make a row of five dots in the center of your rock as shown.

2 Now add two dots above the left and right sides of the dotted row as shown.

3 Finish the heart by adding three dots below the original row, then one dot below that for the bottom of the shape.

4 Use a cotton swab dipped in blue paint to outline the heart as shown. Let dry completely.

5 Your heart is already pretty as it is, but if you want it to have a pixel appearance, use a toothpick to gently scratch between all the rows to turn the dots into squares.

King Trollex

Colors needed:

Dark Blue   Green   Pink   Yellow

1 Use dark blue paint to make a circle on the bottom half of your rock as shown. For a solid color, add a few coats of paint.

2 Carefully add King Trollex's ears with more dark blue paint as shown. Let dry.

3 Use green paint to make two dots for his friendly eyes and add his smile. Then, give King Trollex some spiky hair as shown. Let dry.

4 Now, paint a pink band at the base of King Trollex's hair and the edges of his ears as shown. Use yellow paint to carefully paint two rows of teeth in his mouth. Let dry.

5 Use a marker or toothpick to make pupils. Then, carefully outline his mouth and give his hair some black stripes as shown. King Trollex is now ready to party!

Straight from Techno Reef!

Colors needed:

Yellow   Green

1 To make a sea worm, start with a fat yellow bean shape as shown. You will need two coats.

2 Add green stripes to the worm. Let dry completely.

3 Use a toothpick to scrape away the paint along the edge of the worm to create "legs." Then scratch two dots for its eyes.

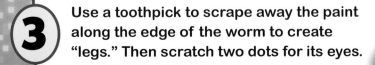

Experiment with different colors and worm shapes!

15

The Country Western Life

Life isn't always easy in Lonesome Flats, but it suits Delta Dawn and the other Country Western Trolls just fine! With plenty of patchwork, cactuses, and cowboy hats, this town is full of country charm. Skedaddle now, and git to painting some rocks!

Delta Dawn

Colors needed:

Peach   Red   White   Pink

Well, dangity-doodly! I love purty things!

1 Use peach paint to make a circle on the lower half of your rock. Make sure you leave lots of room for Delta Dawn's fabulous hair! Add two ears as shown. Let dry.

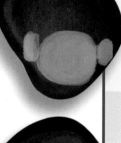

2 Use red paint to make a circle on top of the peach circle as shown.

3 Add two more red circles to give Delta Dawn's hair some shape.

4 It's time to add some magnificent curls! Use red paint to make curls on each side of her face and up top as shown. Let dry.

5 Use a cotton swab dipped in white paint for Delta Dawn's big, beautiful eyes. Then, add two pink circles for her flushed cheeks. Carefully paint a tiny pink nose just underneath her eyes as shown.

6 A cowgirl doesn't go anywhere without her cowboy hat. Carefully paint a little white hat in Delta Dawn's hair as shown. Let dry.

7 Use a marker or toothpick to add the finishing touches: a pretty smile, pupils, eyelashes, texture in her hair, and a little star on her hat. Delta Dawn is ready to square dance!

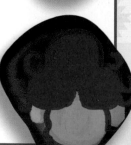

Crazy for Quilts

You may be Pop, and I may be Country, but Trolls is Trolls.

Colors needed:

Magenta   Any other colors

1 Begin your quilt by making a grid pattern with magenta paint as shown. This will create a bunch of squares on your rock.

2 Fill in each square using whatever colors you like. Triangles and diamonds are easy shapes. Let dry completely.

3 Use a marker or toothpick to create black outlines around all the boxes. Then add tiny stitch marks as shown.

Country Cactus

Colors needed:

Green   Purple   Any other colors

1 Use green paint to make a long cactus shape as shown. Add two oval shapes on either side of the long shape. You may need a couple of coats.

2 Connect the ovals to the cactus with more green paint. Now your cactus has arms! Let dry.

3 Carefully add some purple lines to your cactus as shown. They don't have to be exactly the same as you see here. Let dry.

4 Use the purple lines as guides to give your cactus a patchwork design using whatever colors you like. You can clean up the edges of the cactus by scratching the paint off with a toothpick.

Life Is a Symphony

In Trolls Kingdom, classical music flourishes in Symphonyville, a place where golden cherubs float and pennywhistles talk. Ruled by Trollzart, this ethereal land is filled with equally ethereal music. Grab your paintbrush and compose some classical rocks!

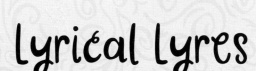

Beautiful!

Classical Rocks

Colors needed in both projects:

Purple   Yellow

1 Paint one side of a rock purple. You will probably need a couple of coats. Let dry.

2 Use a cotton swab dipped in yellow paint to make three dots as shown. These are the bottoms of music notes.

3 Carefully add yellow lines as shown to finish your music notes.

While your yellow paint is still wet, try sprinkling on some glitter. Shake off the excess. Tada! You made beautiful music!

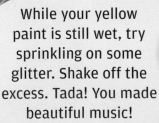

Lyrical Lyres

1 Paint one side of a rock yellow. You will need a couple of coats. Let dry.

2 Use purple paint to make a V shape as shown. Add a dot to the end of each line.

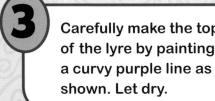

3 Carefully make the top of the lyre by painting a curvy purple line as shown. Let dry.

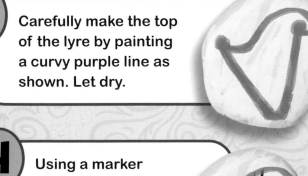

4 Using a marker or toothpick, carefully add several thin strings to the lyre.

Chubby Cherubs

Colors needed:

 Peach **White** **Magenta**

1 Use peach paint to make a circle on the bottom half of the rock. You will need two coats. Add two cute ears to either side of the circle as shown. Let dry.

2 Create the cherub's hair by making several white circles on top of his head as shown. You will need several coats.

3 Use a cotton swab dipped in white paint to make two eyes. Then add a little magenta nose.

After your cherub painting dries, try gluing some cotton balls to his or her head for a classical 'do!

4 Use a marker or toothpick to give the cherub pupils, eyelashes, a pudgy smile, and eyebrows. You can add curly lines to the cherub's hair as well! Adorable!

The Funk Life

Step into Vibe City and you'll begin to feel the funk right away. Everything is groovy in this spaceship city ruled by King Quincy and Queen Essence, Cooper's long-lost parents. Feel the vibe and create some funky rock art of your own!

What's poppin'?

Peace, Love, and Music

Colors needed:

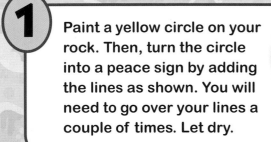

Yellow   Blue   Pink

1 Paint a yellow circle on your rock. Then, turn the circle into a peace sign by adding the lines as shown. You will need to go over your lines a couple of times. Let dry.

2 Carefully go over parts of the yellow lines with blue paint as shown.

Try making a super psychedelic rock using hearts, music notes, and squiggles!

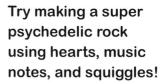

3 Finish your colorful peace sign with some pink lines.
If you want to clean up your peace sign, scratch around the edges with a toothpick.

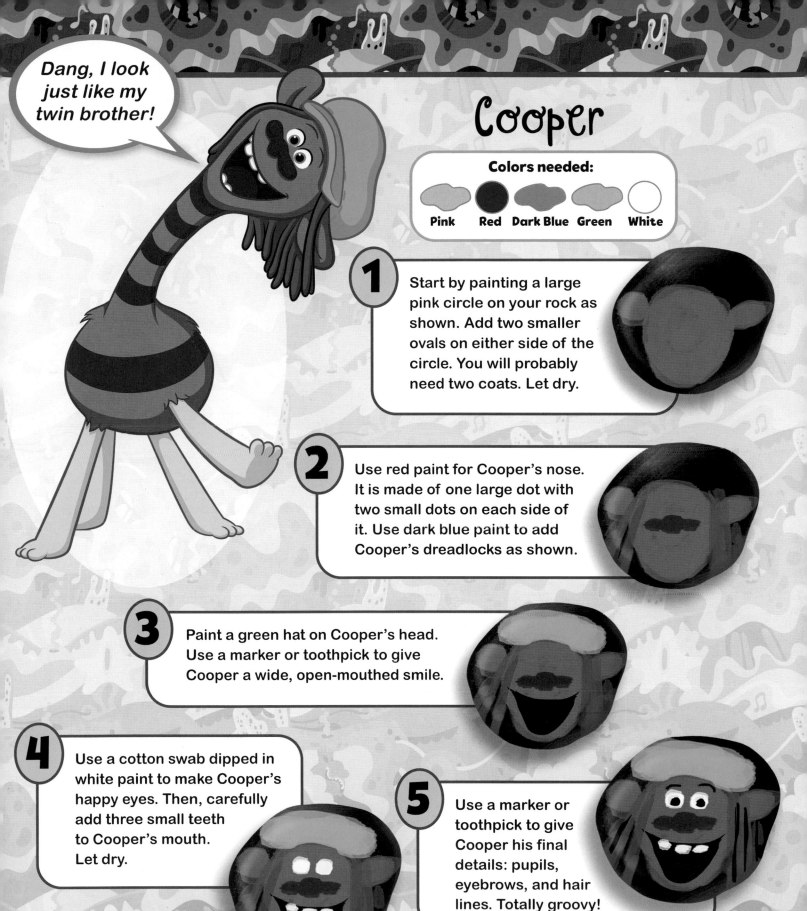

Dang, I look just like my twin brother!

Cooper

Colors needed:

Pink · Red · Dark Blue · Green · White

1 Start by painting a large pink circle on your rock as shown. Add two smaller ovals on either side of the circle. You will probably need two coats. Let dry.

2 Use red paint for Cooper's nose. It is made of one large dot with two small dots on each side of it. Use dark blue paint to add Cooper's dreadlocks as shown.

3 Paint a green hat on Cooper's head. Use a marker or toothpick to give Cooper a wide, open-mouthed smile.

4 Use a cotton swab dipped in white paint to make Cooper's happy eyes. Then, carefully add three small teeth to Cooper's mouth. Let dry.

5 Use a marker or toothpick to give Cooper his final details: pupils, eyebrows, and hair lines. Totally groovy!

Rock Rulez!

The Rocker Trolls have no patience for what they think is silly country music, boring classical, or sickly-sweet pop. It's hard rock all the way! Fierce Queen Barb will stop at nothing to make sure that her beloved rock becomes the only music in Trolls Kingdom. So, get ready to rock these hard rock. . .rocks!

Who knew world domination could be so fun?

Queen Barb

Colors needed:

Dark Gray   **Red**   **White**

1 Using dark gray paint, make a circle on the bottom half of a rock. Then, add two V-shaped ears on the sides as shown. You may need more than one coat. Let dry.

2 Use red paint to make Queen Barb's hairline. It comes to a point in the middle of her forehead. Add a little red nose as shown.

3 Create Queen Barb's spiky mohawk with red paint. Then use a cotton swab dipped in white paint to make two oval eyes above her nose. Let dry.

4 Use a marker or toothpick to give Queen Barb her finishing touches: pupils, eyelashes, arched eyebrows, and a big smirk. Now she's ready to rock!

On Tour

Light Gray Red Dark Blue White

Debbie

1 Use red paint to make an oval on the top half of the rock or the upper part of the skull. You will likely need two coats.

2 Add three red lines beneath the circle. The center line should be longer than the other two lines. This is the bottom part of the skull. Let dry.

3 Use a marker or toothpick to create the skull's eyes and nostrils as shown. Wicked!

1 Use light gray paint to make a circle in the center of the rock.

2 Create Debbie's fur ball appearance by adding lots of brush strokes around the central circle. Let dry.

3 Use a cotton swab dipped in red paint to create two dots for Debbie's wild eyes. Dip the end of the paintbrush handle in dark blue paint to make a tiny nose. Then, paint a big mouth as shown. Let dry.

4 Use a marker or toothpick to make angry eyebrows and the center of Debbie's mouth.

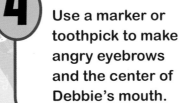

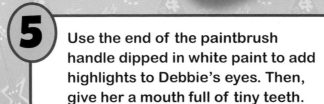

5 Use the end of the paintbrush handle dipped in white paint to add highlights to Debbie's eyes. Then, give her a mouth full of tiny teeth.

Trolls World Tour

Concerts are great places to get together with other people who love the music you do! It doesn't matter if you are a Pop, Country Western, Classical, Funk, or Rocker Troll, show your support with supercool fan buttons, Troll music strings, or hand signs. Grab a rock and express your inner musical Troll!

Music is da bomb!

String Vibes

What is your favorite style of music? Use the Troll strings as inspiration and come up with some string vibes of your own!

Fantastic Fan Buttons

Let your funky flag fly with some cool fan buttons. Here are some ideas to get you started. What does your fan button look like?

These rocks look especially nice with a coat or two of clear coat spray!

Put Your Hands in the Air

Purple   Pink   Yellow

1 Oval rocks are best for this project. Paint a purple oval just above the center of the rock as shown.

4 Using the handle of the paintbrush dipped in yellow paint, add tiny dots to the bracelets.

2 Create the arm and finger shapes with purple paint as shown. Let dry.

5 Finish the hand using a marker or toothpick. Make the outline of the thumb and pinkie as shown.

3 Use pink paint to carefully make three bracelets around the wrist as shown. It might be easier to use the handle of the paintbrush to do this. Let dry.

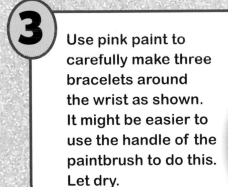

Now that you've gotten the hang of painting Troll hands, try these other options!

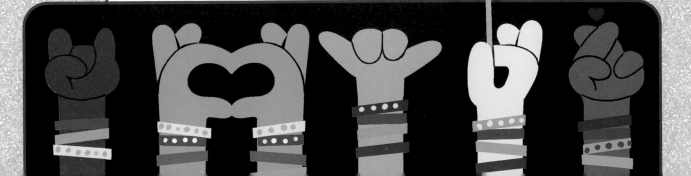

Together in Harmony

In her quest to save music, Poppy learned that differences do matter. They bring fun and excitement to any friendship. After all, you can't harmonize alone. Now Poppy and Queen Barb are buds and life is sweet—just like these colorful, happy rock designs!

Harmonies are cool!

Roller Skates

Colors needed:

Blue   Purple   Pink   Yellow   Green   Red

1 Use a cotton swab dipped in blue paint to make two blue dots on the bottom part of the rock as shown. Let dry. Then carefully paint the purple sole of the boot on top of the dots.

2 Use pink paint to create the boot part of the roller skate. You will likely need two coats. Let dry completely.

3 It's time to decorate your skate! Carefully paint a rainbow on the skate's heel using blue, yellow, green, and red stripes.

4 Use a cotton swab dipped in red paint for the center of each wheel. Then add yellow laces.

5 Use a toothpick to clean up the edges of your skate and to add a line between the boot and sole by scratching away the paint with a toothpick. Now your skate is ready to roll!

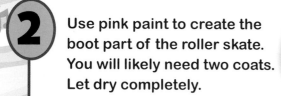
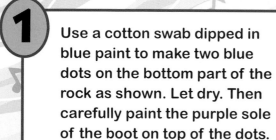

The Sweet Life

Colors needed for both projects:

Yellow Red Blue White Pink Green

Real harmony takes lots of voices.

1 Choose a round rock for this project. Begin by painting the rock pink. You may need two coats. Let dry completely.

2 Starting from the center, make white C-shaped stripes as shown. Make sure you leave some pink showing between the stripes. You may need more than one coat of white. Let dry completely.

Now, try it with green!

1 Use yellow paint to make a circle on the top part of the rock as shown. You will need two coats or more.

2 While the yellow paint is wet, use red paint to make a lollipop swirl as shown. The paint should mix a little while you are doing this. Use blue paint to make the lollipop stick. Let dry.

3 Using the handle of the paintbrush dipped in white paint, carefully add highlights to the lollipop and stick.

You don't need to stick to hard candies and lollipops. Try painting these other sweet treats!

Power Words

Every Troll knows there is power in music, but there is also power in words. They can make someone feel really awesome or super sad. Why not spread some happiness with these rocks that have something positive to say! Keep calm and paint on. . .

Fun Phrases

Here are some ideas to get your started, but you don't have to stick to these colors or words. What do YOU have to say? Say it with colorful rocks!

PEACE

harmony

COOL

YOU ARE A ROCK STAR!

YOU ROCK!

Good Vibes

FUNK

Be Free

Best Friends

MUSIC IS LIFE

BFFs

Do you have a best friend forever? Celebrate your friendship with these rocks that celebrate the two of you!

The more Trolls the merrier!

You will need two rocks for this project. Paint the front and back of one rock with your favorite color, and paint the other rock with your friend's favorite color. Design the rocks any way you like. Use a marker to write your name on one rock and your friend's name on the other.

When the rocks are dry, turn them over and write "Best" on the back of one rock and "Friends" on the back of the other. Keep the rock with your friend's name on it and give the other rock to your friend!

Glitter, Googlies, and Good Vibes

When it comes to crafting, Trolls know it's best to go all-out! *Hair's the thing*. . .everything is better with glitter—and hair! Here are some ideas to take your painted rocks to the next level. Rock on!

Glitter It!

Use a thick layer of paint for best results, and sprinkle glitter while the paint is wet. When dry, gently shake the rock to remove the excess glitter.

Googlies

Add googly eyes or plush hair to your Troll face rocks.

Hair's the Thing!

Instead of painting your trolls' hair, try experimenting with other materials, such as felt, yarn, and tissue paper. Tape or glue the material to the back of the rock to hold in place.

Let's Make Harmony!

Cactuses Rock!

Paint a group of rocks like cactuses, and make a rock garden that even Delta Dawn would love!

Make HARMONY with this fun rainbow rock game. Grab seven rocks and paint them rainbow colors. Paint one letter of the word HARMONY on each rock. Hide the rocks and tell your friends to look for them. Have fun watching them put the rocks together to spell HARMONY.

Help Rock Someone's Day!

Rock painting is fun. The more you paint, the better you will get—— and soon you'll have oodles of beautiful rocks! Unless you have a bunker like Branch, you might need to find homes for your growing collection.

Painted rocks are fabulous gifts that any friend, parent, teacher, or grandparent would love! But did you know that they are also a great way to make a stranger feel *Troll-tastic?* How? Leave cheerful rocks in places where people can find them! Here are some ideas for places to leave your beautiful rocks:

- Leave one on the beach.
- Nestle one in the roots of a tree while hiking.
- Leave one on a mailbox.
- Hide one in a playground.
- Place one in a friend's backpack.
- Leave one on a neighbor's doorstep.

When someone finds your rock, it will make them feel good. It might even inspire them to pass along the happy vibes to someone else. When it comes to making someone's day, YOU can be the rock star!